絲絲森林逗毛毛

Gill Davies 著

Eric Kincaid 繪

洪敦信 譯

三民書局

Haunted House   ISBN 1 85854 775 X

Written by Gill Davies and illustrated by Eric Kincaid

First published in 1998

Under the title Haunted House

by Brimax Books Limited

4/5 Studlands Park Ind. Estate,

Newmarket, Suffolk, CB8 7AU

毛毛有個點子

Fluffytuft Has an Idea

"Nothing is nicer to wake up to than a Spring morning in Silk Wood," says Mrs **Squirrel**.

She **tickles** Fluffytuft's nose with her feather **duster**, but he **pretends** to be asleep and pulls the covers up over his nose.

"Stop it! Go away! I'm still asleep!" he **squeals**, rolling into a ball as the duster **whisks** around his toes.

squirrel [ˋskwɝəl]
名 松鼠

tickle [ˋtɪkḷ]
動 搔癢

duster [ˋdʌstɚ]
名 撢子

pretend [prɪˋtɛnd]
動 假裝

squeal [skwil]
動 尖叫

whisk [whɪsk]
動 輕拂

「沒有比春天早晨在絲絲森林醒來更美好的事了。」松鼠媽媽說。
她用羽毛撢子搔著毛毛的鼻子，可是他卻假裝睡熟了，還把被子拉起來蓋到鼻子。
「不要！走開啦！我還在睡呢！」撢子搔到他的腳趾頭，他吱吱叫著把身子捲成一團。

3

"You won't want any breakfast then," says Mrs Squirrel. "Young squirrels who are fast asleep find it difficult to eat hot toast and **peanut** butter."
Fluffytuft thinks about breakfast and finally **tumbles** out of bed. He **pulls on** his **dungarees** and then settles down to enjoy slice after slice of toast.

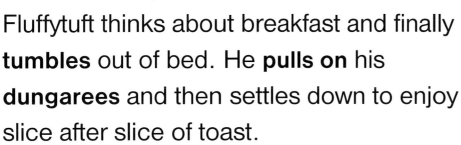

peanut [`pinət]
名 花生

tumble [`tʌmbl̩]
動 滾下

pull on
拉上，穿上

dungarees
[ˌdʌŋgə`riz]
名 斜紋粗棉布長褲

「看樣子，你是不想吃早餐囉！」松鼠媽媽說。「好睡的小松鼠是吃不到熱吐司夾花生醬的喲！」
毛毛想到了早餐，終於滾下床來。他穿上斜紋褲，坐下來享用一片接著一片的吐司麵包。

"Today," **announces** Fluffytuft, "I am going to **lay** an egg."

"Don't be silly," says Mrs Squirrel. "Birds and **snakes** and butterflies lay eggs —— not squirrels."

"I don't care!" says Fluffytuft, putting his plate into the **sink**. "It is Spring. All the birds have eggs in their nests. They have been singing about it every day. Why should they have all the fun?"

announce [əˋnaʊns]
動 宣佈

lay [le]
動 下（蛋）

snake [snek]
名 蛇

sink [sɪŋk]
名 洗碗槽

「今天，」毛毛宣佈說，「我要去下蛋。」
「別傻了！」松鼠媽媽說。「小鳥、蛇和蝴蝶才會下蛋。松鼠可是不會的喲！」
「我才不管呢！」毛毛邊說邊把自己的盤子放進水槽裡。「現在是春天，所有的鳥兒都有蛋在他們的巢裡。他們每天都唱著有關蛋的歌兒。為什麼他們會有這種樂趣呢？」

Rosie Rabbit is waiting outside to play with Fluffytuft.

"Hi, Rosie," says Fluffytuft. "Today I am going to lay an egg."

"Lay an egg!" **laughs** Rosie. "You are silly, Fluffytuft. Squirrels don't lay eggs!"

And she laughs so much she has to sit down and **dab** the tears away with her handkerchief.

"You are very **rude** to **laugh at** me," says Fluffytuft, feeling **cross**.

laugh [læf]
勔 笑

dab [dæb]
勔 輕按

rude [rud]
形 不禮貌的

laugh at
嘲笑

cross [krɔs]
形 不高興的

兔子蘿西正在外頭等著和毛毛一塊兒玩耍。

「嗨！蘿西！」毛毛說。「今天我要去下蛋。」

「下蛋！」蘿西笑著說。「你真蠢，毛毛！松鼠是不會下蛋的。」

她笑得太厲害了，不得不坐下來用手帕把眼淚擦掉。

「妳這樣嘲笑我實在太沒禮貌了。」毛毛很不高興地說。

Fluffytuft **marches** off down the **woodland** path.

It is a wonderful day and soon Fluffytuft **forgets** to be cross.

The sun **beams** down and the **bluebells** smell wonderful. The birds are singing, their nests **snug** full of eggs. Soon Fluffytuft too will lay an egg. He is sure of that.

"I am off to find my very own egg," he tells everyone he meets.

march [mɑrtʃ]
動 行進

woodland [`wʊd͵lænd]
名 林地

forget [fɚ`gɛt]
動 忘記

beam [bim]
動 發光

bluebell [`blu͵bɛl]
名 藍鈴花

snug [snʌg]
副 整潔地

毛ㄇㄠˊ毛ㄇㄠˊ於ㄩˊ是ㄕˋ往ㄨㄤˇ林ㄌㄧㄣˊ間ㄐㄧㄢ小ㄒㄧㄠˇ路ㄌㄨˋ走ㄗㄡˇ去ㄑㄩˋ。
今ㄐㄧㄣ天ㄊㄧㄢ天ㄊㄧㄢ氣ㄑㄧˋ真ㄓㄣ好ㄏㄠˇ，毛ㄇㄠˊ毛ㄇㄠˊ很ㄏㄣˇ快ㄎㄨㄞˋ就ㄐㄧㄡˋ忘ㄨㄤˋ記ㄐㄧˋ了ㄌㄜ他ㄊㄚ的ㄉㄜ不ㄅㄨˋ愉ㄩˊ快ㄎㄨㄞˋ。太ㄊㄞˋ陽ㄧㄤˊ照ㄓㄠˋ射ㄕㄜˋ下ㄒㄧㄚˋ來ㄌㄞˊ；藍ㄌㄢˊ鈴ㄌㄧㄥˊ花ㄏㄨㄚ散ㄙㄢˋ發ㄈㄚ出ㄔㄨ芬ㄈㄣ芳ㄈㄤ的ㄉㄜ香ㄒㄧㄤ味ㄨㄟˋ。鳥ㄋㄧㄠˇ兒ㄦ唱ㄔㄤˋ著ㄓㄜ歌ㄍㄜ，他ㄊㄚ們ㄇㄣ的ㄉㄜ巢ㄔㄠˊ裡ㄌㄧˇ整ㄓㄥˇ整ㄓㄥˇ齊ㄑㄧˊ齊ㄑㄧˊ地ㄉㄜ擺ㄅㄞˇ滿ㄇㄢˇ了ㄌㄜ蛋ㄉㄢˋ。很ㄏㄣˇ快ㄎㄨㄞˋ毛ㄇㄠˊ毛ㄇㄠˊ也ㄧㄝˇ要ㄧㄠˋ下ㄒㄧㄚˋ蛋ㄉㄢˋ了ㄌㄜ。他ㄊㄚ非ㄈㄟ常ㄔㄤˊ確ㄑㄩㄝˋ定ㄉㄧㄥˋ。「我ㄨㄛˇ要ㄧㄠˋ去ㄑㄩˋ找ㄓㄠˇ那ㄋㄚˋ顆ㄎㄜ真ㄓㄣ正ㄓㄥˋ屬ㄕㄨˇ於ㄩˊ我ㄨㄛˇ的ㄉㄜ蛋ㄉㄢˋ。」他ㄊㄚ逢ㄈㄥˊ人ㄖㄣˊ便ㄅㄧㄢˋ說ㄕㄨㄛ。

毛毛下蛋記

Fluffytuft Lays an Egg

Fluffytuft sits by the
waterfall and watches
the **bubbles** dance.
"I like waterfalls,"
he says to **Kingfisher**.
"They make such a
nice rushing-gushing sound."
"Hmmm…" **mutters** Kingfisher, dreaming of
silvery fish to eat.
Rosie Rabbit comes skipping over the bridge
to join Fluffytuft.

waterfall [ˈwɔtɚˌfɔl]
名 瀑布

bubble [ˈbʌbl̩]
名 水花

kingfisher [ˈkɪŋˌfɪʃɚ]
名 翠鳥

mutter [ˈmʌtɚ]
動 咕噥

silvery [ˈsɪlvərɪ]
形 銀白色的

毛毛坐在瀑布旁看水花舞動。
「我好喜歡瀑布呢！」他對翠鳥說。「它們
發出這麼美好、洶湧澎湃的聲響。」
「嗯……」翠鳥正夢想著有銀白色的魚可
吃，低聲咕噥著。
兔子蘿西蹦蹦跳跳地過橋來找毛毛。

"Hi, Fluffytuft," calls Rosie. "Have you found an egg to **hatch** yet?"
She **giggles** and Fluffytuft **frowns**.
"Stop it, Rosie!" he says.
"Don't you dare laugh at me again." He stands up, shaking his tail angrily.
Then Fluffytuft sets off again along the bank.
He is running so quickly he does not see the **twisted** tree roots on the bank and catches his toes on them.

hatch [hætʃ]
動 孵

giggle [ˋgɪgl̩]
動 咯咯笑

frown [fraʊn]
動 皺眉

twist [twɪst]
動 糾結

「嗨！毛毛，」蘿西叫他。「你找到蛋孵了沒？」
她咯咯地笑，毛毛皺起了眉頭。
「不要笑了！蘿西！」他說。「妳敢再嘲笑我！」他站了起來，很生氣地搖著尾巴。
然後毛毛又沿著河岸出發。他跑得很快，根本沒注意到河岸上糾結的樹根，腳趾頭就被它們鉤住了。

Yow! Bump! Splash! Fluffytuft tumbles down into a pool. "Oh dear!" he **groans**. "I am **completely** wet through and covered in mud."
And then he sees the egg. It is resting in a **hollow**. It is smooth, **shiny**, and white with **speckles**. No-one is sitting on it.
"Hello, little egg," says Fluffytuft. "Would you like to **belong** to me? I can take good care of you."

groan [gron]
動 呻吟

completely [kəmˋplitlɪ] 副 完全地

hollow [ˋhɑlo]
名 坑洞

shiny [ˋʃaɪnɪ]
形 閃爍的

speckle [ˋspɛkl̩]
名 小斑點

belong [bəˋlɔŋ]
動 屬於

唉喲！砰咚一聲！水花四濺！毛毛跌進了一個池塘裡。
「天啊！」他呻吟著說。「我渾身都溼透了，還沾滿了泥巴。」
接著，他就看到了那顆蛋。它躺在一個坑洞裡。它的表面光滑、閃閃發亮，白色帶點兒斑點，而且沒有其他的動物坐在它上頭。
「嗨！小蛋兒，」毛毛說。「你願意屬於我嗎？我會好好照顧你的。」

19

Fluffytuft is so excited to find an egg of his very own that he does not **realize** it is not an egg at all. It is a **pebble** —a beautiful **egg-shaped** pebble.

Fluffytuft builds a **mound** of grass and moss and then lays the egg **carefully** on top. "There," he says. "Now I have laid an egg." Fluffytuft sits on his nest all afternoon and waits for his egg to hatch. But nothing happens.

realize [`riə,laɪz]
動 了解

pebble [`pɛbl̩]
名 小圓石

egg-shaped [`ɛg,ʃept]
形 蛋形的

mound [maʊnd]
名 堆

carefully [`kɛrfəlɪ]
副 小心地

毛毛好興奮能找到一顆真正屬於自己的蛋，以致於沒有注意到它根本就不是一顆蛋！它是一顆小圓石——一顆漂亮的、蛋形的小圓石。
毛毛用草和苔蘚做了個小土堆，然後小心翼翼地把蛋放在上頭。
「好啦！」他說。「現在我下了顆蛋囉！」
整個下午，毛毛都坐在他的巢上，等著他的蛋孵化，可是卻一點兒動靜也沒有！

At last Fluffytuft jumps off the nest and **peers** inside. But his egg has **disappeared**. Has it hatched already and run away? Big tears are rolling down Fluffytuft's face when Rosie Rabbit **arrives** and asks, "Why are you crying?"

"I found my egg and then I hatched it, but now it has run away!" **sobs** Fluffytuft.

Rosie **plunges** her **paws** deep into the nest and pulls out his egg.

peer [pɪr]
勔 凝視

disappear [͵dɪsəˈpɪr]
勔 消失，不見

arrive [əˈraɪv]
勔 到達

sob [sɑb]
勔 啜泣

plunge [plʌndʒ]
勔 插入

paw [pɔ]
名 掌

最後，毛毛只好跳下來，往巢裡探頭，可是他的蛋不見了。難道它已經孵化出來，跑掉了嗎？大顆的眼淚滾落毛毛的臉蛋兒，這時，兔子蘿西來了。她問：「你為什麼在哭呢？」

「我找到了我的蛋，然後也把它孵化了，可是它現在卻跑掉了。」毛毛啜泣著。

蘿西將手掌深深地插入巢裡，把他的蛋拿了出來。

"Oh, Fluffytuft," she laughs. "Your egg is a pebble. It is so **heavy** it has fallen to the **bottom**."

Now Fluffytuft laughs too. "What a silly squirrel I am!" he squeals, rolling on the ground.

The friends **paint** the pebble and give it to Mrs Squirrel. She says, "You know, if it wasn't for these **patterns**, you might think this was an egg. Now why are you two giggling?"

heavy [ˈhɛvɪ]
形 重的

bottom [ˈbɑtəm]
名 底部

paint [pent]
動 畫，著色

pattern [ˈpætɚn]
名 圖案

「喔！毛毛啊！」她笑著說。「你的蛋只是顆小圓石嘛！它因為太重，所以掉到底下去了。」
現在連毛毛也笑了。「我真是隻笨松鼠啊！」他笑得滾到地上吱吱叫。
他們兩個把這顆小圓石畫上圖案，送給松鼠媽媽。松鼠媽媽說：「你們知道嗎？如果沒有這些圖案，你可能會誤以為它是一顆蛋呢！咦～！你們倆在笑什麼啊？」

救難小福星

Heather S Buchanan著　本局編輯部編譯

15×16cm／精裝／6冊

在金鳳花地這個地方，住著六個好朋友：兔子魯波、蝙蝠貝索、老鼠妙莉、
鼴鼠莫力、松鼠史康波、刺蝟韓莉，
他們遇上了什麼麻煩事？要如何解決難題呢？
好多好多精采有趣的歷險記，還有甜蜜溫馨的小插曲，
就讓這六隻可愛的小動物來告訴你吧！

 魯波的超級生日

 莫力的大災難

 貝索的紅睡襪

 史康波的披薩

 妙莉的大逃亡

 韓莉的感冒

老鼠妙莉被困在牛奶瓶了！糟糕的是，她只能在瓶子裡，看著朋友一個個經過卻沒發現她。有誰會來救她呢？

（摘自《妙莉的大逃亡》）

網際網路位址　http : // www. sanmin. com. tw

ⓒ 毛毛有個點子／毛毛下蛋記

著作人　Gill Davies
繪圖者　Eric Kincaid
譯　者　洪敦信
發行人　劉振強
著作財
產權人　三民書局股份有限公司
　　　　臺北市復興北路三八六號
發行所　三民書局股份有限公司
　　　　地址／臺北市復興北路三八六號
　　　　電話／二五〇〇六六〇〇
　　　　郵撥／〇〇〇九九九八——五號
印刷所　三民書局股份有限公司
門市部　復北店／臺北市復興北路三八六號
　　　　重南店／臺北市重慶南路一段六十一號
初　版　中華民國八十八年十一月
編　號　S85518
定　價　新臺幣壹佰捌拾元整
行政院新聞局登記證局版臺業字第〇二〇〇號

ISBN　957-14-3072-0 (精裝)